BY JAKE MADDOX

illustrated by Tuesday Mourning

text by Val Priebe

Librarian Reviewer
Chris Kreie
Media Specialist, Eden Prairie Schools, MN
MS in Information Media, St. Cloud State University, MN

Reading Consultant
Mary Evenson
Middle School Teacher, Edina Public Schools, MN
MA in Education, University of Minnesota

STONE ARCH BOOKS
www.stonearchbooks.com

Impact Books are published by Stone Arch Books
151 Good Counsel Drive, P.O. Box 669
Mankato, Minnesota 56002
www.stonearchbooks.com

Library of Congress Cataloging-in-Publication Data
Maddox, Jake.
    Running Rivals / Jake Maddox; illustrated by Tuesday Mourning.
    p. cm. — (Impact Books. A Jake Maddox Sports Story)
    ISBN 978-1-4342-0778-4 (library binding)
    ISBN 978-1-4342-0874-3 (pbk.)
    ISBN 978-1-4342-2504-7 (pbk.)
    [1. Running races—Fiction. 2. Competition (Psychology)—
Fiction.] I. Mourning, Tuesday, ill. II. Title.
PZ7.M25643Ru 2009
[Fic]—dc22   2008004292

Summary: Amy hurt her knee in a race. Now she's back on the team,
but will have to get her confidence back in order to compete.

Art Director: Heather Kindseth
Graphic Designer: Kay Fraser

Printed in China

102009
005577

TABLE OF CONTENTS

CHAPTER 1

BACK TO THE TEAM

The walls of Dr. Smith's exam room were mint green. They were covered with certificates, diplomas, and drawings that looked like they'd been made by little kids.

My dad was sitting in a chair, reading a magazine. I was sitting on the exam table, wishing that Dr. Smith would hurry up.

All he had to do was walk in, look at my knee, and tell me whether it was healed enough for me to run again.

I was a mid-distance runner. I ran the 400. A lot of people think the 400 is the toughest race in track. It's 400 meters, one lap around the track, running as fast as you can.

I usually got first place. I only got second place if my biggest rival, Madison Palmer, was running.

But you can't run at all if your knee has been hurt, like mine was. I had hurt my knee almost two months earlier, at the very beginning of the season.

There was a knock at the door and Dr. Smith walked in. "Hi Amy! Hi Mr. Reid! How are you two doing?" he asked.

Dr. Smith shook my dad's hand. Then he got out an orange rubber hammer and started tapping on my knee.

"How has your knee been feeling?" he asked me.

"It feels normal," I told him. "Can I get back to my team?"

Dr. Smith laughed. "That's why I love sports medicine," he said. "Athletes always want to get better so fast."

He looked at my chart and continued, "Well, I've looked at all of your X-rays and scans. Your knee seems to be healed. I'll let you go back, but you have to promise not to overdo it."

"I'll take it easy," I promised. "Anyway, we don't have a track meet until Tuesday."

"Okay, Amy," the doctor said. "You'll have to start slowly, and make sure you're stretching and resting your knee after runs. Good luck on Tuesday." He shook my hand.

"Thanks, Dr. Smith!" I said.

When we left the clinic, I was so excited that I jumped for joy. But my knee gave a little shake. I suddenly felt nervous.

What if my knee wasn't better enough? What if I didn't have any speed?

The next meet was only five days away. What if I wasn't ready?

CHAPTER 2
SCARED

"Wow, I didn't think he'd let you run again so soon," Dad said as we headed home. "Are you excited?"

"Yeah," I said. "Do we have an ice pack at home? I need to make sure to use it on my knee every time after I'm done running."

I was trying to change the subject. I didn't want to tell my dad how scared I was.

"Yes, we do. Hey, is everything okay?" asked Dad.

"Yep," I replied.

"Good," said Dad. "Don't worry, honey. Tuesday's meet will be here before you know it."

When we got home, I put my backpack in my room, and then went into the dining room for dinner. For a few minutes, the only sounds were the clinks of forks and knives on plates.

"Natalie, how was school today?" asked my dad between bites.

"It was good," my older sister replied. "The yearbook is going really well."

"Great!" Dad said.

"Amy, what did the doctor say?" Natalie asked.

I felt my face turn red. I could hide my nervousness from my dad, but not from my sister. I looked down and answered, "I can go back to practice. Dr. Smith said I had to be careful, though."

I concentrated really hard on cutting my chicken so I didn't have to look at her. Natalie could always tell if I wasn't telling her something by looking at my face.

"I think I'll go for a run after dinner," I said. I loved running. It always made me feel better. I guess it helped me think things through in my head.

"I found a new trail in the park, and I don't have any homework," I added.

"Just don't push too hard," said Dad. "I'll have the ice pack ready for you when you get back."

I went down the hall to my room and changed my clothes. I was really worried about my knee as I slipped out the back door. I walked across the street and into the park, stretching as I went.

When I got to the beginning of the trail, I began to jog.

CHAPTER 3

A DIFFERENT TRACK

I usually ran at the track at school, but so did all of my teammates. I didn't want them to see me if I had to stop or if I was slow. I just wanted to run. So I headed to a different track than usual.

Concentrating on my breathing and form, I ran up a little hill. Just on the other side, the trees cleared and I could see a tennis court, two basketball hoops, and a track.

I started to jog down the hill toward the track. Then I noticed a flash of purple under the track lights.

It was a girl. She was tall and had a long brown ponytail. She was wearing purple and gold, the colors of our rival school, Emeryville.

I stopped and waited just out of sight. When the girl rounded a corner, I realized who she was. It was Madison Palmer. Why was she running there?

Madison was my biggest competition for the 400. She and I had been running against each other since fifth grade, and she almost always beat me. And to make matters even worse, she'd been running next to me when I'd gotten hurt earlier in the season.

The meet was in Emeryville. I had been in lane one, the closest to the inside of the track. Madison had been in lane two. When the starting gun went off, I had burst out in the lead. From the corner of my eye, I could see that Madison was keeping pace with me.

As we rounded the second turn into the last straightaway, I had glanced over at Madison.

That was the biggest mistake I could have made.

When I looked away, I stepped just a little too close to the edge of the track. My shoe got caught on the plastic between the grass and the asphalt.

I felt a pop, and then a lot of pain in my left knee.

Somehow, I managed to finish the race. I placed last. And then my dad took me to the hospital. I hadn't run since.

A woman's voice snapped me back to the present. "You had a good kick there at the end," the woman called to Madison. The woman was standing just off the track. "1:05," she went on. "That's your best time all year."

"Really?" said Madison, panting slightly. "Great!"

"It's getting late," said the woman. "Why don't you jog a couple of laps to cool down, and then we'll go."

One minute and five seconds? I couldn't believe it. That was a great time. I had never run the 400 that fast.

"Okay, Mom," Madison said.

I sat for a while. I just listened to Madison's footsteps.

Her mom was right. It was getting late. As I turned to jog back up the hill, my knee gave another shake. My heart sank. Madison was running a very fast 400 and I could hardly jog without pain.

Dad had the ice pack waiting for me when I got home. It was so cold I had to close my eyes and grit my teeth as I put it onto my knee.

Then Natalie walked in. "Hey, Amy. How was your run?" she asked.

"Fine," I said. I looked away.

"It wasn't fine," she said, frowning. "When you're ready to talk, you know where to find me."

CHAPTER 4

OUT OF PRACTICE

The next day was Friday. I was really looking forward to getting back to practice. It seemed like the school day lasted forever.

As soon I got out to the field after school, I found Coach Joseph.

"Amy! I'm so glad to have you back," said Coach Joseph. "How's your knee feeling?"

"It's okay," I said, looking away.

The truth was that my knee was sore from my run the night before. I didn't tell my coach. I didn't want him to worry.

"Are you ready for practice?" Coach Joseph asked.

"Absolutely," I said.

"Great," he said. Then he blew his whistle. "Okay, team," he called. "Let's do two laps and stretch." He blew his whistle again and we started running.

After we stretched, my knee was still sore, but not really painful. It seemed okay.

Then we split up. The people who did field events, like the discus or high jump, went to practice their throws and jumps. The long-distance runners took the three outside lanes of the track and started running.

Those of us who started our races with starting blocks (the 100-meter, 200-meter and most of the 400-meter runners) each had a partner. The other person stood on the block so that it wouldn't move. Then, after the race started, they took the block off the track.

My partner was a girl named Katie. We grabbed a set of blocks. Katie said, "Amy, I'm so glad you're back. I've had to practice starting with Coach Joseph. He makes me so nervous!"

"Oh, Katie, that's too bad," I said with a laugh. "I'm glad to be back too. Is it okay if I go first?"

"Sure," said Katie.

I set up the blocks at the starting line and adjusted them.

Katie stood on the back of the blocks. I put my feet up against the blocks and got down on one knee. She waited as I lined my hands up to the starting line.

When my hands were in place, Katie said, "On your mark! Get set!"

I pushed up so that my knee was off the ground. But just before she yelled, "Go!" I shot out of the blocks and ran a few yards. That was a false start. In a real race, that would have disqualified me.

We tried a few more times, but I just kept false starting. I was so afraid of starting slow that I couldn't relax and wait.

"Don't worry about it, Amy. You're just out of practice," said Katie.

"Yeah, that's probably it," I said. "Your turn."

I got up. The starting position was making my knee sore anyway.

When Katie was done practicing her starts, we were rounded up with the rest of the runners. We were going to do a drill called the Caterpillar.

We all ran in a line, one behind the other, around the track. Every so often, the last person in the line would sprint to the front.

It felt so good to be back, running next to my teammates. It was a beautiful, sunny day for my first practice back.

As we ran, I timed my breathing with my footsteps, in for two and out for two. I just listened to the sounds of our footsteps on the ground and let myself be happy to be back, running along the track.

But the longer I ran, the more my knee hurt. I was glad when Coach Joseph finally blew his whistle.

"Great practice today, everyone," he said. "Now, you all know we have two meets next week, on Tuesday and Friday. So get some rest this weekend and get ready for a big week. Have a great weekend!"

CHAPTER 5
NATALIE'S IDEA

I woke up late on Saturday morning. Natalie was in the kitchen when I went to find something to eat.

"Are you ready to tell me what's bothering you, Amy?" she asked. She looked at me over her glass of orange juice.

I knew she was trying to help me feel better. I just wasn't ready to talk about my fears.

"I'm fine, Natalie. Really," I said.

My sister raised her eyebrows. I could tell that she didn't believe me.

"What?" I asked her.

"Well," she said, "you haven't been able to talk about running lately without looking away from me. It's your favorite thing. Why are you acting like you don't like it anymore?"

"I do still like it!" I answered.

"Then what's the problem?" she asked again. "Amy, you know me. I'm not leaving you alone until you tell me."

Great, I thought. Natalie could be really stubborn when she wanted something.

"Okay," I said. "I had a hard time with starts today. I'm sure I was just kind of out of practice, though, so now will you leave me alone?"

"Okay," said Natalie. "I need to shower and think. I'll come find you when I'm done."

"You do that," I said under my breath. "I'm going for a run," I told her.

I wasn't normally so crabby with my sister, but the more I thought about the upcoming meets, especially Friday's meet against Madison, the more scared I got. I didn't see how anyone could help me, so I just didn't want to talk about it at all.

* * *

When I got home, I was limping a little from the soreness in my knee and not feeling any better. I took some medicine to help my knee. When I came out of the bathroom, Natalie was waiting for me. She had a big smile on her face.

"Why are you so happy?" I asked, wiping my sweaty forehead with a towel.

"Because I had an idea," she replied. "What do you think about calling Coach Joseph and asking to use a set of blocks for the weekend?"

I stared at her. What did I think? "Natalie!" I shouted. "That's a great idea!"

CHAPTER 6

THE OLD AMY

I gave Natalie a sweaty hug while she screamed and tried to get away.

"I get it! I get it!" she cried, laughing. "You like the idea! Now get away from me and call your coach."

"Do you think he'll mind if I call him?" I asked nervously.

Natalie shook her head. "I doubt it," she told me. "He will be glad that you want to work hard over the weekend."

I grabbed the telephone. Coach Joseph answered on the second ring.

"Coach?" I said. "It's Amy."

"Good morning, Amy," said Coach. He sounded worried. "Is anything wrong? How's your knee?"

"It's fine, I'm fine," I said. I tried to ignore the nervous feeling in my stomach when he mentioned my knee. "I'm really sorry to call you at home, but I was hoping I could borrow a set of blocks for the weekend. Is that okay?"

"Oh! Sure!" Coach said. "That's a great idea!"

"It was Natalie's," I said honestly. I looked over to see her smiling at me. "Can you meet us at the school in twenty minutes?" I asked.

"Sure thing," Coach Joseph said. I gave Natalie a thumbs-up.

"Okay," I said. "See you then."

* * *

When we got home, Natalie and I planned our afternoon. She said, "I can hold your blocks for you. I was also thinking I could bang on a pan with a spoon for the starting gun."

I laughed. "We usually just say 'go,'" I told her, "but if you want to bang on a pan, you go right ahead."

Natalie blushed a little. "Right," she said. "I guess I got a little carried away." Then she laughed too.

We went to the back yard. Natalie searched for a flat spot while I stretched.

"Let's get you started," she said when she found a spot.

My first few attempts went as badly as they had at practice the day before. I false started every time. Every time, I was up and past the string we were using for a starting line before Natalie ever said go.

"Amy, just wait for it," she said after the fifth try, sounding frustrated. "It's not even a real race!"

"I know that, Natalie," I said, trying to be patient. "But you have to practice like it's the real thing."

Natalie sighed and stepped off the block. She put her hands on my shoulders. "Amy, I don't know what's really bugging you, but you're a good runner. You've worked so hard," she said.

Then she looked me in the eyes and said very slowly, "You can do this. I know you can. Just take a deep breath and try to relax."

The knot in my stomach, which had been getting worse with every start, loosened a little. I smiled at my sister.

Natalie and I worked until almost dinnertime. My knee was sore by the time we finished, but not like it had been the day before. Toward the end, my old timing had started to come back. I was still a little bit too quick out of the blocks, but I felt more confident.

"That's better," said Natalie as we walked inside. "Almost like the old Amy."

CHAPTER 7

THE FIRST MEET

I was nervous about my first meet, and Tuesday came fast. Madison's school wasn't going to be at the meet, though, so at least I could relax about that.

The meet was at our school. After classes let out, Katie and I took our time changing into our uniforms and making our way to the field.

"How are you feeling, Amy?" asked Katie as we changed. "Are you nervous?"

"A little," I said. "It'll be good to get this meet over with so I can concentrate on Friday."

"Well," said Katie, "I'm really glad you're back."

I smiled and said, "Thanks, Katie. I'm really glad to be back. I can't believe how much I missed all this hard work!"

We laughed. Then we walked toward the team camp in the middle of the field.

Soon the meet started. I jogged between starting lines, sand pits, finish lines, and jumps to root for my teammates. Race after race finished.

Finally, it was time to find out which lane I would run in. The official with the clipboard was a short, gray-haired lady with bright pink shoes.

"Name, please," she said, glancing at my jacket to see the name of my school.

"Amy Reid," I replied.

"You're in lane three today, Amy," said the official.

I walked over to the starting line and began to stretch.

A few minutes later, a voice called over the loudspeaker, "Last call for the girls' 400-meter run. All runners to the starting line!"

I found an out-of-the-way patch of grass and took off my wind pants and jacket. I had goosebumps on my arms and legs.

It was so cold out. I walked to lane three and hopped up and down, trying to keep warm.

An official yelled, "On your marks!"

I lowered myself to the asphalt. I pushed my right foot, then my left foot, up against the starting block.

"Get set!" yelled the official.

I tried to breathe, but I was so nervous and cold that it wasn't easy. I just kept telling myself to wait for the starting gun.

BANG!

The gun went off. I pushed myself as hard as I could out of the blocks.

After a few seconds, my left knee gave that familiar shake. I felt like I was running in slow motion.

All of the runners rounded the first turn close together. Then we headed into the straightaway.

The runners in lanes two and six were ahead of me.

I was still in third place as we hit the second turn. My knee was tightening up with each stride.

There were less than a hundred meters to go. I fell back to fourth place.

Fifty meters to go.

I used all the strength I had. I passed the runner in lane one.

With twenty-five meters left, the girl in lane one passed me again. I could hear my teammates cheering me on.

I pushed myself as hard as I could for the last ten meters, passing the runner in lane six at the very end. I finished the race third.

I was out of breath and hurting. Soon, Katie came running up with my jacket and pants.

"Thanks, Katie," I said, grateful to be warm again. "What was my time?"

Katie looked away. "1:10, Amy," she said softly.

My jaw dropped. I had never run so slowly! One minute and ten seconds was only about four seconds slower than my normal time, but in a race as short as the 400, four seconds is like forever!

I bent down to untie my laces so that Katie wouldn't see the tears in my eyes. There was no way I would ever be ready to run against Madison on Friday.

CHAPTER 8
ANOTHER IDEA

When I got home, I went straight into my room. I was hoping for some privacy, but my dad knocked on my door.

"Can I come in?" he asked.

"Why?" I asked. I wasn't in the mood to talk to anyone.

"I want to talk to you, honey. I want to make sure you're okay," he replied.

"All right," I said, sighing. "It's open."

Dad walked in. "Sweetie, will you come into the kitchen and talk to me?" he asked. He looked worried. I got up and followed him.

"What's going on?" he asked.

"I ran a 1:10 tonight," I said. "I have never run that slowly!" I wanted to cry again, and my voice shook a little.

"I know," my dad said. "But I feel like there's something else. You haven't been yourself since we got back from Dr. Smith's office."

He put his hand on my head. "Spill it, kid," he said. "Tell your old dad what's on your mind." Dad looked at me. We were both quiet for a long time.

Finally, before I could change my mind, I told him everything.

I told him about my first thoughts of nervousness, about worrying about my knee, about seeing Madison in the park, about my false starts, and finally, about my really huge fear that I wouldn't be ready for Friday's meet. It was the final meet of the year. It was a really big deal.

"Madison has had two months of practice more than me," I finished. "She's been running faster than I've ever run. Today I tried as hard as I could and ran slower than ever."

Dad looked at me for a few seconds. He seemed to be thinking hard.

"Have you talked to Coach Joseph about any of this?" he asked finally.

"Dad, I haven't talked to anyone about any of this," I said.

"Oh, honey. I don't know what to tell you," Dad said with a sigh. "All you can do is your best. And you still have Friday's meet, right? I'm sure your slow run tonight was just you being nervous. Plus, you're still getting back into shape."

"Yeah," I said.

My dad didn't seem to understand how upset I was. I needed to talk to Natalie. My sister was always really good at solving problems.

"Dad?" I asked. "I need to talk to Natalie," I said. "No offense or anything," I added quickly.

"I understand, Amy. I'll go get her for you." Dad said as he stood up. He even looked a little relieved.

Soon, my sister walked into the kitchen.

"Okay, Amy," Natalie said, sitting down next to me. "Dad told me everything, and I have an idea."

She took a deep breath. Then she went on, "Why don't you go to the track in the park and talk to Madison? Maybe you can practice with her or something."

That wasn't exactly what I had in mind. "Are you kidding?" I asked.

"No, I'm not. She's just a girl who likes to run, like you are," said Natalie.

I sat for a few seconds to let the idea sink in. "Will you come with me?" I asked finally.

"Yeah," she said. Then she smiled. "I'm not running, though."

I laughed. "Deal," I said. "We'll go tomorrow after dinner."

CHAPTER 9

MY BIGGEST COMPETITION

The next day, Natalie picked me up after practice. "Are you ready for tonight?" she asked.

"No," I said.

"Amy!" exclaimed Natalie. "We talked about this yesterday. Did you change your mind?"

"No," I said again. "Madison just makes me really nervous. She always wins."

"I bet she's just as impressed by you," said Natalie.

But I didn't think so.

* * *

After dinner, I put on my running clothes. Ten minutes later, Natalie and I were heading for the track.

As soon as we reached the track, I saw Madison. She was sprinting through the last hundred meters of a lap.

I started to turn around, but Natalie held onto my elbow and guided me toward the track.

Madison stopped running as we walked up. She squinted at us through the fence. "Amy Reid? Is that you?" she asked.

"Yeah," I said, surprised. "How do you know my name?"

Madison laughed. "Because you're my biggest competition!" she said. "What are you doing here?"

"Well, I live near here," I told her. "This is my sister, Natalie." Natalie and Madison smiled at each other.

I took a deep breath and went on, "So anyway, I was running near the track last week and saw you practicing." I looked at my sister for help.

"Amy had a rough meet last night. I suggested she come to ask you for some advice," Natalie said. "I mean, I know you're on different teams and everything, but . . ." She stopped. Madison had started to blush.

"Are you kidding?" asked Madison. "I should ask Amy for advice!"

I was shocked. "About what?" I asked.

"Your form!" Madison said. "Your form is always so perfect."

Then Natalie said, "If you two are going to practice, you should really get started."

Madison and I went to the starting line. We decided to run the first lap in our own styles, so that we could see the differences side-by-side.

We were really close for the first half, but I was in the lead.

I noticed that Madison's elbows seemed to fly out from her body a little. It was almost as if she was having trouble keeping her arms in close like you're supposed to.

We went around the second turn. That's when Madison sped up.

I tried to keep up with her, but I was out of energy. Plus, my knee was bugging me again.

Madison beat me by about two meters. That's a lot in such a short race.

After we caught our breath, I asked, "What's your secret?"

"I used to try to sprint the whole thing, but I was always so wiped out by the end. My coach suggested I try it a different way," Madison explained. "If you run a little slower than normal for the first half of the race, you can speed up for the second half and pass everyone." She shrugged. "It works really well."

I thought for a minute. "Okay," I said. "Let's run it again. This time I'll try it your way."

We ran another lap. That time, I actually beat her!

After we cooled down a little, I gave Madison some tips on keeping her elbows in close to her body. "See, I just pretend I'm on one of those ski machines, you know?" I told her. "Like on TV? It takes some getting used to, but keeping your elbows in really makes a difference."

Finally, I noticed that the sun was below the trees, so we decided to call it a night.

"See you Friday!" called Madison as Natalie and I headed back down the trail toward home.

"See you then!" I yelled back.

I felt happier than I had in days.

CHAPTER 10

PERSONAL BEST

Friday morning was chilly and sunny. But by the time we changed and boarded the bus to drive to the meet, the sky had clouded over, the wind had picked up, and the rain was coming down in sheets.

It was the worst possible weather for a track meet. All of my good feelings from Wednesday night disappeared.

The drive to Emeryville didn't take long, but it felt like forever.

The rain had let up a little by the time we got there, but the wind was still blowing. To make matters worse, it seemed like the rain and cold were making my knee stiff.

I was sitting with Katie when Coach Joseph walked back and sat down in front of us. "Amy, how's your knee feeling?" asked Coach Joseph. "Because if anything could hurt your knee again, it would be running in this weather. So if you don't want to run today, you don't have to."

He saw the look on my face and quickly added, "But if you want to run, I think you should stay on the bus where it's warm and dry until it's your turn."

Soon, we arrived at the school. Little butterflies started to form in my stomach. I was so nervous.

This meet was a really important meet. Anyone who finished first or second in their event would compete in the State Finals.

Usually, I'd have run in many meets before this point in the season. But this season, I'd been out for two months. The finals at the end of the season had really snuck up on me.

The time seemed to fly by as I waited for my race. Soon, Coach Joseph was telling me what lane I was going to run in. Then he led me off the bus.

I was in lane one. It was the same lane of the same track I had been hurt on.

I took my position in the lane. Madison was right next to me, in lane two. We smiled at each other.

"On your marks!"

I crouched down and faced forward.

"Get set!"

I pushed my toe as close as I could to the starting line without actually touching it.

BANG! The starting gun went off.

I concentrated all of my thoughts and effort on keeping up with Madison.

When we hit the second curve, Madison put on a burst of speed. I was surprised to find myself right next to her.

I was using Madison's method for running. So far, it was making a big difference. We were neck and neck. My knee hurt a little, but I ignored it. Then Madison pulled ahead. I pulled ahead of her for a few meters, but I couldn't keep my lead.

Suddenly, it was over. Madison had won.

For a second, I felt really disappointed. Yet again, Madison Palmer had beaten me.

But then Katie came running over. "Amy!" she called, sounding excited. "You ran a 1:05!"

"Are you serious?" I asked. I felt shocked. That was my fastest time ever. "Did I really?" I couldn't believe it. How had I run a 1:05 with a healing knee?

"Yeah, you really did," a girl's voice said.

I turned around. It was Madison. "Congratulations," I told her. "You were great."

Madison smiled. "You were too! Personal best, right? Your best time ever?" she asked. "That's got to feel great!"

I smiled back. "Yes, it was," I admitted. "It feels pretty good."

Madison laughed. "Wait till the next meet," she said.

"You wait till the next meet," I joked. "Then my knee will be totally healed, and I'll be some serious competition!"

Everyone cheered as the official read our times into a microphone. I could see my dad and Natalie in the stands, jumping up and down.

"You already are serious competition," Madison said, smiling. "I can't wait till the next meet."

A GREAT FEMALE ATHLETE:

"My goal was to be the greatest athlete who ever lived." Those were the words of **Babe Didrikson Zaharias**, and she may have achieved her goal.

Babe was born **Mildred Ella Didrikson** in Texas in 1911, a time when women were supposed to get married, stay home, and take care of the children. Even women who were athletes were supposed to be ladylike, and **Babe** was not ladylike. She wore pants and played on teams with boys because there were no leagues for women.

She said she was nicknamed **Babe** after baseball legend Babe Ruth, because of the long-distance home runs she hit while playing baseball with neighborhood boys.

In 1930, **Babe** was offered a job playing basketball. During that time, she became interested in track and field.

BABE DIDRIKSON ZAHARIAS

In that same year, **Babe** won four national track and field events. In 1932, she won a national track and field championship all by herself, scoring a total of 30 points. That was eight points more than the second-place team. She broke world records in the javelin throw, the 80-meter hurdles, the high jump, and the baseball throw.

Babe was voted the Greatest Female Athlete in the first half of the twentieth century by the Associated Press. She was also voted Female Athlete of the Year six times, once for track and five times for golf which she took up later in her life.

Babe died of cancer in 1956, while still in the prime of her life. Some experts say that there has not been a female athlete like **Babe Didrikson Zaharias** since.

ABOUT THE AUTHOR

Val Priebe lives in Minneapolis, Minnesota with her two crazy wiener dogs, Bruce and Lily. Besides writing books, she loves to spend her time reading, knitting, cooking, and coaching basketball. Other books that Val has written in this series include *Full Court Dreams* and *Stolen Bases*.

ABOUT THE ILLUSTRATOR

When Tuesday Mourning was a little girl, she knew she wanted to be an artist when she grew up. Now, she is an illustrator who lives in Knoxville, Tennessee. She especially loves illustrating books for kids and teenagers. When she isn't illustrating, Tuesday loves spending time with her husband, who is an actor, and their son, Atticus.